BABY SHARK

Doo Doo Doo Doo Doo Doo

Art by John John Bajet

Cartwheel Books
An Imprint of Scholastic Inc.
New York

Watch out for a dance guide at the end of the story!

ISBN 978-1-338-55605-6 (Trade)
ISBN 978-1-338-56461-7 (Fairs)
10 9 8 7 6 5 4 3 2 1   18 19 20 21 22

Printed in the U.S.A.   40
First printing, December 2018
Designed by Doan Buu

A long, long time ago, there lived a . . .

Baby Shark, doo doo doo doo doo doo.
Baby Shark, doo doo doo doo doo doo.

Baby Shark, doo doo doo doo doo doo.
BABY SHARK!

Mama Shark, doo doo doo doo doo doo.
Mama Shark, doo doo doo doo doo doo.

Mama Shark, doo doo doo doo doo doo.
MAMA SHARK!

Daddy Shark, doo doo doo doo doo doo.
Daddy Shark, doo doo doo doo doo doo.

Great White Shark, doo doo doo doo doo doo.
Great White Shark, doo doo doo doo doo doo.
Great White Shark, doo doo doo doo doo doo.

GREAT WHITE SHARK!

Grandma Shark, doo doo doo doo doo doo.
Grandma Shark, doo doo doo doo doo doo.

Grandma Shark, doo doo doo doo doo doo.
GRANDMA SHARK!

Here they come! Doo doo doo doo doo doo.
Here they come! Doo doo doo doo doo doo.

Here they come! Doo doo doo doo doo doo. **HERE THEY COME!**

Shark attack! Doo doo doo doo doo doo.
Shark attack! Doo doo doo doo doo doo.

Shark attack! Doo doo doo doo doo doo,

SHARK ATTACK!

Swim real fast! Doo doo doo doo doo doo.
Swim real fast! Doo doo doo doo doo doo.

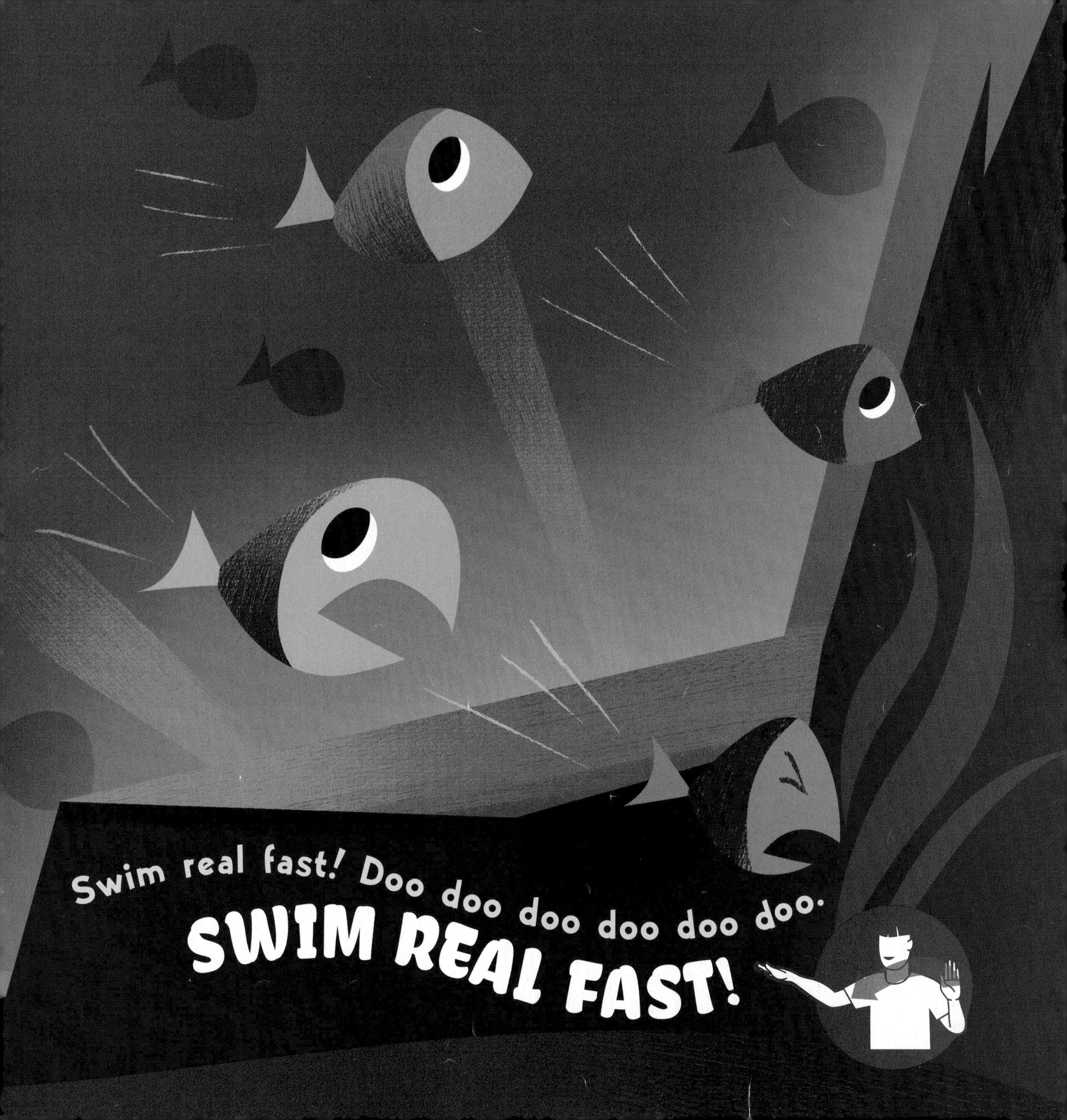

Swim real fast! Doo doo doo doo doo doo.

SWIM REAL FAST!

Safe and sound! Doo doo doo doo doo doo.
Safe and sound! Doo doo doo doo doo doo.

Safe and sound! Doo doo doo doo doo doo.

SAFE AND SOUND!

That's the end! Doo doo doo doo doo doo.
That's the end! Doo doo doo doo doo doo.
That's the end! Doo doo doo doo doo doo.

BABY SHARK DANCE!

BABY SHARK!

Pinch two fingers together like a shark mouth.

MAMA SHARK!

Snap both hands together like a bigger shark mouth.

DADDY SHARK!

Snap arms together like an even bigger shark mouth.

GREAT WHITE SHARK!

Snap one arm and one leg together like the biggest shark mouth.

GRANDMA SHARK!

Snap two closed hands or fists together like a toothless shark mouth.

HERE THEY COME!

Bring two hands together in a point on top of the head like a shark fin.

SHARK ATTACK!

Spin arms around the head like a whirlpool.

SWIM REAL FAST!

Wave arms back and forth in a swimming motion.

SAFE AND SOUND!

Use the back of one arm to wipe your brow.

THAT'S THE END!

Do a wiggle dance with fingers pointing up.